# BRIDGE OVER SEASONED WATER

## A PARANORMAL WOMEN'S FICTION HOLIDAY NOVELLA

### MURKY MIDLIFE WATERS
### BOOK FIVE

## JB LASSALLE

**MIGHTY OAK**
PUBLISHING SERVICES

# CHAPTER 1

Frieda wasn't listening to me.

It didn't matter what I did, nothing was working. I jabbed at it, tried the swipey action, and even did the thumb and forefinger nonsense Iris always used on her phone. I rotated the damn device every direction I could think of. Nothing worked.

My work tablet was done for the holidays, and there was not a thing I could do about it.

Maybe I'd get a new one for Christmas or as a present to myself. A twinge of melancholy made me bite my lip. When I'd been with Daniel, he'd gotten me a new device every year. Always the latest whatever, even though I did little more than scroll through social media and text people.

It was nice, though, having a thing that worked immediately when you asked it to. Frieda here was probably ten years old. It had taken days to get it updated and the right apps installed, just to run booking. Having something new and shiny would be nice.

When Max slammed the door to Bridge House, I jolted, and Frieda crashed to the floor. On a gasp, I scooped it up and inspected it for a crack. Nary a scratch. I breathed a sigh of relief. Say what you will for new and shiny, at least Frieda was reliable.

"Sorry boss ... er, bosses." Max offered me his goofiest grin as he sauntered into the sitting room, which we'd taken to using as a front office. "Wind caught it."

"Mm-hmm." Max slammed that door twenty times a day, wind or no. The House had taken to bracing itself whenever he walked towards it, which meant I got tense twenty times a day. I gritted my teeth, forcing my tone to be much nicer than I felt. "Please try and be careful."

"Will do, ma'am." Max plopped himself into the oversized recliner by the window, draping one leg over the chair's arm like he was in a dorm. "The Gundersons are checked out. Bridge House is officially empty for the first time since Halloween!"

The last of our guests were gone, but he wasn't technically right. Empty was a concept long forgotten in the past few months. Even the quiet pleasure of me and Ruth swinging on the porch in the evenings was gone. Since our opening on Halloween, Bridge House had become a revolving door of check-ins and check-outs.

Word of the waystation being back up and running had gotten out much more quickly than I'd expected. I kind of wish I'd done a test run before I officially opened the doors. For the past six weeks, I'd stumbled my way through a number of firsts, and not always gracefully. To my credit, I was just living up to my brand.

I am probably the only awkward mermaid on the planet. Then again, I haven't met them all.

"No more guests until the day after Christmas." I closed the tablet and docked it to charge. "I won't miss looking at you tomorrow, Frieda."

"Why do you call it Frieda?" Max hauled himself off the recliner and brushed shell dust off the windowsill. Each time Pop visited, he stashed more of his handmade collection wherever he thought guests might see them.

I was glad that Pop came around more often, but he really needed to use more reliable shells. Or actual shells, rather than bits of glass or rock that got everywhere. Or better glue that kept them attached.

"I had a friend named Frieda. She was just as sassy as that tablet." I stuck my tongue out at the inanimate object then turned my back on it like the petulant child I was.

"Had? Did something happen to her?"

"Nope. We just ... lost touch." The sharp sting of betrayal pulsed in my throat, but I swallowed it down and brushed my hands like I could erase the subject. "Want to help me cycle the linens before we call it a day?"

"I got them, Ms. Misty. Why don't you swing on the porch for a few?"

In his short time here, Max had become much more than a groundskeeper and porter. He could tell when I was run down or overwhelmed, or when I needed a moment to myself. He'd even taken to helping in the cafe when he sensed Sam and Kitty could use a break.

It was like he belonged to the island, which was probably true. He was a good kid; however, there was a glint in his eye that I didn't like. A hint of mischief that pinged my bullshit radar.

"What's going on?"

Max bit his lip, and like usual when his emotions got the best of him, his inner wolf peaked out. His canines elongated, and his fingernails sharpened. He cast his eyes to the floor, scratching at a spot behind his pointy ear. It had been a fight and a half to get rid of his fleas, but the itch was a habit that persisted.

"Not a thing, Ms. Misty. It's pretty outside, and you've had a rough week. Thought you might want a moment on the porch is all."

Something was up, and I was in no mood for it. But Max was right. I'd been out of sorts for weeks, and a moment of solitude on the porch would do me some good.

I shouldn't have been out of sorts. All in all, things were good, if a bit hectic. The B&Bers were content, reviews were strong, and I was getting the hang of the oddness that was being caretaker of a mystical waystation. I'd even managed to find a nice balance between magic and mundane.

Sure, it involved a lot of excuses to the guests who had no clue what was happening, and a lot of placating Bridge House who had a mind of her own, but I was doing it.

I had a nice routine. Norbert, Iris, and I had breakfast every morning. I swam every evening. And a few nights a week, Dimitri and I explored our new relationship.

It was the holidays. I had a full day off. I should have been happy.

But as I opened the door to Bridge House and saw the surprise that awaited, I had one thought: Bah, humbug!

# CHAPTER 2

*S*ometime this morning, while I was seeing guests out
and visiting the stragglers in the cafe, a giant yule tree,
decorated with cherubic faced angels and ornaments bigger than
my fists, had materialized on the porch. It was so tall that the
rainbow star alighting the top of it scraped against the overhead
paint.

Icicle lights lined the grand staircase leading up to the porch.
They glittered blue even in the light of day. I stomped off the
stairs, ignoring the soothing breeze that greeted me, and turned to
take the entire house in.

The same icicles hung from my balcony. I shielded my eyes to
get a better look, and they flickered gold, sending my shoulders all
the way up to my ears.

"What did you let them do to you?"

The lights glowed brighter, as if Bridge House was preening.
Wreaths unfurled in the windows and a garland of ivy trailed itself
along the gutters. A thousand fairy lights twinkled from just
about every nook and cranny visible.

"What the hell happened to it?" Dimitri's footsteps shuffled
behind me, and he slid an arm around my waist. I leaned into it,

the thrill of his touch taking me away from the horror before me. But only for a moment.

"Apparently the holidays threw up all over my house."

"I think she looks good." He chuckled, a deep rumble in his chest that reverberated against my back. "It's better than Thanksgiving."

I hmphed. He had a point, at least she was embracing *this* holiday. I loved Thanksgiving, and after an epic battle with Sam, he'd agreed to let me do the cooking for everyone.

I'd polished the long table in the dining room so deep I could see my reflection. Sam and Kitty made themselves scarce while I stuffed the turkey and whipped the potatoes. I spent the day sweating over the stove. I dug out the oldest china set I could find, handwashing each piece and creating a table that Pinterest would envy.

I was swelling with pride. My found family gathered at the table. I lifted my camera to snap a picture.

And the bitch turned off the power.

Apparently, Bridge House and I disagreed on which holiday was better.

I was screaming at the walls when Charley pulled in. The house was so happy to see my daughter that she turned the power back on so we could eat, but only after Charley talked her into it.

By then, the food was cold and the turkey dry. Still, it ended up being a delightful evening. Maybe one of my favorites since I'd returned to the island. And even though Charley was newly single, and eyed Max a shade too long across the table, it was good to have my girl back and people who loved and accepted me to break bread with.

Charley was spending Christmas with her father and his new wife, who allegedly glowed as she neared her third trimester. Not that she could glow brighter than the damn house.

"Bah, humbug." I turned to Dimitri, capturing his lips with mine and pressing myself closer. We were in public, and it was the middle of the day, but I was hopeful that a few minutes of necking in the parking lot would distract me from my sour mood.

He wrapped my hands in his and brought them to his chest.

"What's going on, Misty? You've walked around sour for weeks." A wry grin lifted his lips. "I'm supposed to be the grumpy one in this relationship."

"I'm just tired." My heart ticked a bit harder at that word. *Relationship.* Plus, when was Dimitri the one to stop our makeout session to talk about emotions?! I pulled my hands away and fiddled with the hem of my shirt. "I don't like Christmas."

Dimitri put one finger to my chin and lifted until our eyes met.

"Can you tell me why?"

Part of me wanted to. We'd been friends before we'd become lovers, and he was still someone I knew would accept me without judgment. I'd tried to talk to Iris about it the night before, when we'd drank wine and fed Norbert marshmallows, but every time I brought it up, it got lodged in my throat.

But it wasn't just the one thing I didn't want to bring up. I had a litany of worries keeping me up at night. So, I chose an easier one to talk about.

"I can't find Talia's Star. I've searched the whole damn house, and it's nowhere to be found." I whirled to face the house and pointed an accusing finger at the steps. "She knows where it is. I can sense it. But she won't tell me." I took another step forward and raised my voice. "I'm on to you, missy. Don't for a second think this stupid light festival will distract me."

Dimitri crossed his arms across his chest, lifting one eyebrow. I hated that he was amused with my outburst, and I hated even more that he could look so hot while I was so annoyed.

"What is it really?"

"That is *it*, really." I kept my eyes averted and fought the urge to play with my hands. Did he know me so well already? "Jean Lafitte and I made a deal, and things are going well here. If he shows up—"

7

"When Jean Lafitte returns, we will handle it." Dimitri pulled me close and planted a kiss on my forehead. "Troll trumps ghost, remember?"

My lips twitched, and I let my shoulders relax. It wasn't fair that I was casting all my frustrations on Dimitri. Deep down, I wasn't as worried about Lafitte as I pretended to be. Having a giant, hot troll in your corner really does wonders for your confidence.

He didn't need to know I hated Christmas. He didn't even need to know why. Troll not only trumped ghost ... troll was a nice distraction. I ignored the house flashing brighter in the corner of my eyes and leaned into him.

"Misty." He pulled away, furrowing his brow as he gazed toward the cafe.

Kitty rushed down the steps and scampered toward me as fast as her short legs could manage, mirroring the worried expression Dimitri wore.

"Misty, we need you up there. Something's happening to Abraham Lincoln."

# CHAPTER 3

*W*alking into the cafe and finding the ghost of Abraham Lincoln sitting at a corner table was the last thing I wanted to deal with. Lincoln waved me over, a timid smile on his face, and I shuffled over trying to keep my face neutral.

As I neared him, I recognized the weathered hat and the penny tattoo on his wrist. Like a visit from the past, there sat Walter, my first brush with the supernatural when I'd returned to the island.

"Hello, Misty. So nice to see you again. It seems you are well."

"Walter, I've wondered where you went off to. You look great." I stared down at my napkin in case the lie was really obvious. Walter didn't look great at all. When he used to frequent the island, he'd hovered between spectral and human. No matter his form, though, there'd been an air of peace and knowing about him that was missing now.

The Walter in front of me looked like he'd been through a war. His beard was stark gray, his skin yellow, and he wore the unmistakable darkness of fear like a shadow under his eyes. His chuckle sounded the way I remembered; however, and he templed his fingers like he used to when he recited the Gettysburg Address.

"You are a fantastic liar, Misty. And while I appreciate it, we both know I do not look well."

I lifted my eyes to his, relieved that I didn't have to pretend.

"What's happened to you, Walter?"

Very human tears welled in his eyes and trailed down his face, cutting a line through the makeup I'd never noticed he wore.

"Do you remember the lovely morning we chatted, right here at this table? You asked me about my time as a Lincoln impersonator, and if I remembered coming to the cafe."

I braced myself as the tingle of the supernatural flitted along my spine. I'd felt this moment a lot in the past few months, in the instant where someone who thought they were mundane realized there was an entire world they didn't know about. It was when I knew to step in and help them to either embrace or reject their alternate form.

It buzzed through me like a finger in a light socket, but this was a different kind of familiar. There'd been a few times someone had decided to straddle both worlds. Not like me, where I'd embraced my decision not to choose. Rather, they'd denied what they were and lived in a sort of limbo. It was a different sensation. A tingling like I'd sat on my foot too long, and it had fallen asleep, but deeper. Like a buildup of pressure that would never be released.

"I remember, Walter. You told me about your rousing speech on the bridge and the lovely Mary Todd. Then you walked away." I swallowed the dry lump in my throat. "Where did you go, Walter?"

"To the bridge, of course. To meet my friends. They weren't there. I stumbled ..." Walter turned to look over his shoulder, toward the path that led to North Bridge and the dense forests of Bridge Island that only Max knew well. His figure faded until I could barely see him and turned a pale green like it was sick. He shook his head and gripped my hands with the sudden horror of a man facing the end.

"I believe I might have fallen off the bridge. That would be a long fall, and I cannot swim." His long fingers squeezed mine until my skin turned blue, but I couldn't escape his grasp. "Yet here I am. Right?"

"Yes, Walter, here you are." I sucked my breath in as the prickling grew, sapping the energy from my body. Even my teeth tingled. Though irrational, I was certain if he continued to hold onto my hands, he could suck the life out of me. "But, Walter, you *did* fall off the bridge many years ago. You were drunk and stumbled right over the edge.

"You've roamed the island ever since." His eyes hollowed, and his head elongated until I was staring at a misshapen form, barely a ghost but definitely not human. "I'm sorry, Walter."

His wide, empty mouth let out a wail. The other patrons in the cafe turned toward it, cocking their heads like they heard a sound far away. But I wrenched my hands from his clutch and planted them on my ears as the howling filled my head. A deep throb erupted behind my eyes, and the cafe and everything around us darkened into nothing.

"Save my spirit, Misty!" He held his fingers to the space where his face had been. Scaly and grotesque, they bent backwards as though his bones were breaking. "I'm running out of time."

I had the sensation of water filling my lungs, but my mermaid disappeared, and my chest closed in on me. The pain overwhelmed me, like a slow cutting of a thousand knives. I clawed at my throat, unable to breathe. I opened my mouth to call for help, unable to make a sound.

Then I snapped my head up, tipping the chair and landing with a hard thud on my back. Kitty's frightened face filled my vision. I stumbled to my feet and surveyed the cafe. Walter was nowhere to be found, but his tinny cries for help still rang in my ears like the lingering clash of cymbals.

# CHAPTER 4

"*W*alter didn't know he was a ghost?"

"We thought he did. He always looked so serene." Kitty worried the tip of one of her orange ponytails. "What's wrong with him?"

"I don't know." A deep sigh pulled itself out of me. I gestured toward the kitchen, and Kitty followed me to Sam. "Hey, Sam? Was Walter a guest here at the B&B? You know, until he ..." I made a diving gesture with my hands.

"Yup. His entire troupe was one of the last before we closed up the rooms. They held services back in his hometown, if I recall. Always found it odd his spirit stayed here." Sam sprinkled flour on the marble countertop and spread dough as we talked. A bowl of diced apples, drenched in cinnamon and butter, waited to be piled into the crust he kneaded like an expert. My mouth watered a little in anticipation, bringing a swamp water aftertaste that gave me chills.

"Has anyone seen him on the island anywhere other than the cafe."

"I don't know, Misty. Isn't that your job?" He pressed the dough into a pie pan with his thick, nimble fingers, glaring at me over his nose. "Any other questions for me, or can I get back to work?"

I flinched at the retort. After the Thanksgiving debacle, Sam wouldn't let me in the kitchen, which meant he was spending his afternoon preparing a feast he'd have to wake up at the crack of dawn to finish.

I'd been there. When I was married and Charley was young, I had worked into the night countless Christmas Eves to make sure Daniel's Christmas dinner was perfect. I'd set up gifts from "Santa" and baked cookies, all the while fighting my own exhaustion and asking for nothing in return.

In hindsight, it had been silly of me to take it on myself instead of asking for help from my family. At the time, I'd told myself it would make them happy. And to be fair, it did. But surely there was some middle ground where I could have enjoyed the holiday, too?

I shook off the old me, who was selfless to a ridiculous degree because she was afraid to want anything for herself. My nerves were on edge, and now I had a Walter problem to contend with, but Sam was like my grumpy uncle, and I didn't want him mad at me.

"Sam, I would really love to help you with that."

"It's okay, pet. Kitty and I are going to make an evening out of it." His face softened, and a small smile lifted his wiry beard. "If it helps, when Walter was here, he stayed in the President's Suite."

"Of course, he did." I stomped up the stairs. My emotions teetered between being annoyed with Walter for picking today to do this and worrying that he might be too far gone to save. By the time I'd reached the top step, I had added a heaping dose of guilt to my emotional baggage.

Bah, humbug.

I sensed a presence in the President's Suite before I reached the door and flung it open.

"Damnit, Walter, couldn't you have realized you were a ghost the day after Christmas?"

But it wasn't Walter in the room.

A woman sat on the bed, facing the large windows that over-looked the forest. Her hair reached down to her waist. She was a ghost, no doubt about it, but there was something else about her that I couldn't put a finger on.

"Hello?" She didn't answer or turn. I did a mental count in my head, ensuring my ever-doubting brain that all the guests had checked out already. I couldn't picture a woman of her height or body here in the past few days. She ran one hand across the bedspread as if lost in thought.

"Ma'am, can I help you?" The house pushed against my back with such force that I stumbled over my toes. As I neared the bed, I planted my feet on the floor. I didn't like this, the sense of famil-iarity washing over me or the way the house suddenly swelled with joy.

She turned halfway, and her profile was my profile. She opened red-painted lips and sang a lovely song, both foreign and nostalgic. A rush of memories from my youth returned. Not the young-girl years, when I was desperate for a mother's love and took care of the house and had dreams of its future.

No, her song took me farther back. Touching the haziest of memories from a time I was scarcely able to form them.

I found myself sitting on the bed beside her, taking a very real hand and placing it to my heart. She was a blur between me and my shield of tears. I joined her song. A song I'd known when I was too young to question the world. A song of love and belonging.

A song that sent a name to me. Nerida.

"Grandma?"

The ghost of my mother's mother stroked my cheek, and I pressed myself into her palm. Her smile filled my vision.

"Hello, Little Fin. It's been too long."

"That it has." Her hand was as wrinkled and soft as a favorite blanket. The woman who had cared for me beside Aunt Ruth, and who had died when I was five. Here she was, sitting on my bed. The house let out a happy sob. "Of all the magic on this island, I did not expect to see you again."

"Surely you didn't think I'd miss this special occasion? She chuckled, and it was a laugh I remembered. "You've just begun to experience the wonder of Bridge Island." Her smile turned down at the sides, a show of sadness that put me on edge. "Though I fear there are still lessons you will insist upon learning the hard way."

"I gotta be me." I'd meant it as a joke, but my tone came out hollow and flat. "What are you doing here?"

"I'm here for you." Her words echoed in my brain. My heart beat cold in my chest. My body began to shake. Had I drowned in the cafe in place of Walter? Was I a ghost, too? Or had I gone through all this just to die on Christmas Eve?

What the hell, man?

"Grandma, if you've come to take me to the other side, I'm going to have to object. I don't really want to go yet. I'm just now figuring out this whole life thing. Things are mostly well here; it's loud and chaotic, but it's pretty. And I have a boyfriend. I know that word is weird and juvenile, and, okay, maybe not a reason to plead to stay alive, but I have an Iris, too. And sure, I'm grumpy right now, but usually—"

Nerida held her hand up.

"Relax, dear one. I've not come for you in that way. I've come to help you see things more clearly. I've come to soothe this pain." She rested her hand upon my chest. "It's time you face yourself, Little Fin."

Ugh, she was right. Something was empty inside me, some hollow piece that hated this time of year and was fighting any festivity. I resented my duties; I'd been sour with my friends. In fact, I'd been a grinch since Thanksgiving.

I'd been just like Scrooge. Demanding and grumpy. Which could only mean ... oh, no.

"Are you, like, the ghost of Christmas past?"

"Something like that." Nerida ran her hands down my arms, pulling my fingers to her lips with an enigmatic smile.

"So, I'll be visited by more of you tonight?" I bit down on the inside of my mouth and closed my eyes, feeling out the house's emotions. It was an empty sensation, like the house was withholding itself from me. Was this a practical joke? Could a house play a practical joke?

I shut my eyes, as much from fatigue as disbelief. I'd have to work on myself tonight. Face all those lingering issues I was still holding onto. Admit to everyone why today was—

"I am the second, dear one." Her words jolted me back, and I opened my eyes to face her. Sadness darkened her features. "The first is your lost wanderer."

My grandmother was from the past. Did that make Walter the ghost of Christmas present? It was too much. As certain as I'd been earlier that I was drowning on dry land, I was equally certain I was not up to the task of intense self-reflection on Christmas damn Eve.

"Is there any way I could learn this lesson after the holidays? I am fresh out of empathy. I've been giving it away in droves over the past few months, and I'm exhausted." I pulled my shoulders to my ears and let them drop. My whole body dropped with it. "I'm exhausted, Grandma."

She opened her arms, and I sunk into them, resting my head against her shoulder. As she hummed her siren song, my eyes closed again. It was strange. Her song didn't lure me anywhere. Not toward the water or the land. Her song settled me in place. When it stopped, I could hear my heart hammering in my chest.

"Fulfilling your purpose gives you the energy you need, darling. If you're worn out, perhaps it's because you are so busy worrying about making mistakes that you've chosen to focus on controlling the future." Her soft laugh was the first drop of honey in warm tea. "Why take on such an impossible task, Little Fin?"

She turned me to face her, meeting my eyes with a look of compassion.

"Walter only has tonight. And he only has you. Help him, dear one, and let whatever ghosts still haunt you do their best." She poked her finger to my nose. "I'm certain you can manage it."

Then my grandmother disappeared, just as Walter had, leaving me alone with arms outstretched toward an unmet hug and my thoughts in disarray.

# CHAPTER 5

$\mathcal{T}$wenty minutes later, I had a mini search party assembled on the porch. Aunt Ruth bounced on the swing, as if we were about to embark on an adventure. Both Kitty and Sam wore identical expressions of concern, while Iris and Max watched me steadily. I smiled at Iris, to let her know I was okay, and she lifted one sculpted eyebrow as if she didn't believe me.

Which was fair. I didn't believe me, either.

"How was Nerida?" Ruth asked me, as if my long-dead grandmother had stopped in for a quick chat rather than crossing over to the land of the living to Jacob Marley me.

"She looked like I remembered. Ruth, can you stay close in case she returns, or Walter does?"

"Aye aye, captain." She mock-saluted me with a giggle. It was getting dark, and though more lights had spawned in the time I was upstairs, and I was fairly certain you could see Bridge House from space, I didn't want her wandering the island at night.

"Sam and Kitty, you'll take the south half. Max, Dimitri is waiting for you by North Bridge. Can you two search the forests and the northwest of the island? You guys can cover the most ground the fastest."

Max gave me a quick nod, then trotted down the stairs and toward the lit path to Dimitri's, shifting as he went.

"Just one more check of my pie." Sam side-eyed me on his way back to the kitchen.

"You know, he's been baking all day," Kitty told me as she brushed past. As if I didn't feel bad enough.

"What if he left the island?" Iris crossed her arms and leaned against the house. "What if he's crossed the bridge?"

"It's possible," I told her. "But I'm not sure he can anymore. Let's wander down the levee and let Norbert know what's happening. Then you and I can follow the shore. Hell, I'll swim if I have to." I glared out toward the bay. "Maybe he's under water."

Iris lifted her chin but didn't move. I shifted my glare to her.

"What?"

"What happens if we don't find him?"

I tapped down on the frustration pressing itself against my chest, resisting the urge to snap my words out.

"He'll probably exist in the in-between forever. And since I can still feel him and talk to him, even if he's all misshapen and grumpy, I'd like to avoid that." I tapped my foot when she showed no signs of moving. "Are we doing this? I still have another haunting to endure."

# CHAPTER 6

"*W*alter!" I cupped my hands over my mouth like a hand-made megaphone.

"Why are you bellowing?" Norbert swished his tail against his favorite rock when we approached.

"What the hell is that?" I pointed in horror at the tiny Santa cap angled on his head strapped underneath his long chin.

"It's my favorite time of year." Norbert snapped his jaws, reminding me of his power. "I think it looks festive."

It looked ridiculous, but I wasn't about to tell him. No matter how far gone I was, pissing off an alligator seemed like a bad idea. Especially one that was on a marshmallow diet and probably craving meat.

"We're looking for Walter." Iris crossed her legs and sat beside him. "He disappeared from the cafe today after Misty fumbled the delivery of his ghostliness." I glared at Iris without replying, sneering when she lifted her mouth into a grin. "He's the ghost of Christmas present for our siren Scrooge over here."

"I didn't fumble the delivery," I bit out. "Everyone thought he knew he was a ghost."

"You mean he didn't?" Norbert turned his head to me, the

soggy Santa cap jiggling with the movement. "How could he not know that?"

"Thank you." I removed my clothes and retrieved one of the bags I kept around the island. I fiddled with the bag's handle, an involuntary smile tugging at my lips. Dimitri had been the one to start the practice, one of his many moments of silent thoughtfulness. "I don't know how to do this."

"You do this every day, Misty." Iris brushed dirt off her skirt and took the bag from me, shoving my shirt into it. "You've already got the bikini on. Just slide into the water. I can walk the shores."

"Not that." I plopped to my butt in the sand and swung my arms toward the island. "All this. I don't know how to do it."

"Bullshit." Her words were harsh, but her tone was soft as she lowered herself next to me. "You've gone through this before. Well, not this exact scenario. You've been the caretaker for two months now." She bumped her shoulder to mine. "Maybe I don't tell you enough, but you're rocking it."

"It's true." Norbert slid off the rocks and toward us. As his thick body moved from side-to-side, the cap tilted, yet managed to remain on top of his head. "We're all really proud of you."

It was cooler than summer, and Norbert was wearing a Christmas cap, but this night still reminded me of the one not long after I'd arrived. I leaned back to take in the stars, sitting in their friendship. A nagging urge to move rose to my throat, but I tried, at least for a moment, to suppress it.

I had to help Walter, that was true. But Nerida said I had to deal with my own crap, too.

"Thanks, guys. I know I've been, well, a bitch lately. I keep expecting the bottom to drop out." I let all my breath out, then sucked it back in. "When I say I don't know how to do this, I don't mean being caretaker. Or even being mermaid."

I stood and paced the shore as that urge lifted further.

"I don't know how to be human. To be, you know, happy without finding something to worry about. There's always something sitting here." I turned to face my friends and gripped my stomach. "And today is the worst."

Iris and Norbert exchanged a glance. Iris nodded like an entire conversation had happened between them.

"We know what today is, Misty. Did you think we'd forget?"

"Kind of." My pulse rose and I gnawed on my lip. "It's been so long, and there was so much I forgot. I kind of hoped you had, too."

"No way." Norbert flicked his tail like I'd insulted him.

"We weren't sure if you remembered at first," Iris stood and up and jabbed at my shoulder. "But then you got all snippy with everyone without telling us why, and we figured you knew."

A piece of the weight I'd been carrying over my heart chipped away from my chest, letting me breathe a shade easier. Maybe I didn't need to worry about the future solo. Not when I had others who wanted to help me.

I laughed out loud. I kept convincing myself I was alone, even while begging for solitude.

"We love you, friend." Iris's voice was thick with unshed tears as she pulled me into a quick hug. "So, let's find Walter, fix him up, then celebrate."

I returned her hug, patted Norbert's back, and headed toward the water. The transition was like a blink, and I marveled that six months earlier I didn't even know I had a tail.

Yet here I was, diving deep without a second thought. I'd figured out how to be a mermaid. I'd figured out how to be a caretaker. I'd figure the rest out, too.

# CHAPTER 7

*T*he water was like a cool stream on a hot day, and though Walter was short on time, I took a few moments just to enjoy the feel of it on my skin. Bayou water wasn't exactly the cleanest, but tonight it was no different than the bluest sea in the Bahamas. Since deciding to straddle both worlds, it was rare for me to crave a swim. But this week, my swims had bordered on manic, filling a need I hadn't understood until now.

I circled the island three times at breakneck speed, just to work up a sweat and release the pain I'd held onto without realizing. It occurred to me that this was what healing actually felt like. I kept hoping it would be a switch that I could flip, and that remembering my purpose on the island had helped me find the lever.

But growth was more like a dial, turning itself lower and higher as I moved through life. True healing came in ugly, uneven layers. Uncovering dark pockets of pain that pop up unexpectedly and facing them when they made their presence known, even if it was inconvenient.

I could reach a point where I barely thought of Daniel but still feel the sting of his betrayal at the holidays when my daughter had to choose between us. I could find my place on the island where I was born and still be hurt that Pop had taken me away from my legacy just as I was figuring it out. I could accept that my mother left because of a call too strong to be denied and still be bitter that she'd abandoned me.

I could turn the dial one way or the other without fixing it into place. Maybe that was being human after all, not the experiencing of trauma, but the moving through it into something unknown.

I slowed my pace, widening my search to the opposite end of North Bridge. The New Orleans side, where Walter might have fallen. The terrain was different here, an area I hadn't explored much as Norbert and I preferred to swim out into the open.

I flicked my tail to go deeper, inspecting the seabed. I wasn't sure what I would find. Not a body, I thought with a shudder. But at the very least, new shells for Pop. With no sign of Walter and my hand full of trinkets, I rounded the bridge and approached the surface.

The Christmas lights of Bridge House lit up the night sky, making stars all but disappear. And in the hint of their lights, something shimmered underneath North Bridge.

It moved with grace, a pink pearl in the night.

Another mermaid.

She smiled at me as I drew closer, and though her smile was a bit vapid, I knew it. In fact, I knew her. Long hair the color of rust, now streaked with gray. Round eyes bluer than the sky. Sharp features like mine, marred with age.

She had the same crow's feet I had. Her lips were a little thinner, just like mine. Dark brown spots, not quite freckles but borne of too much sun, mimicked the ones splattered across my cheeks.

My first thought was this was the ghost of Christmas future, and I was at once annoyed and in awe that the island had somehow manifested a vision of me twenty-five years from now.

But this wasn't me.

The tail was the tip-off. My tail sparkled like gems in shades of azure and green that brought to mind strength and resilience. The mermaid in front of me had a tail like a rose pearl. Its shine was deeper. More like it was lit from within. More like a glow than a glitter.

And the vivid shades of pink that adorned the tips were unmistakable.

They were the same pink as the hideous rose wallpaper that Bridge House had finally let me get rid of.

They were the same pink as the many dresses I'd found in the old-fashioned wardrobe in the bedroom I now called mine.

They were the same pink as the unused lipstick in the faded white vanity I'd moved into the attic.

It was a pink I'd long associated with my mother.

And it was her face staring at me. Her carefree eyes roamed my tail with curiosity. Her hands gave me a timid wave as if we were strangers.

This wasn't the ghost of Christmas future. Not technically. Because it wasn't a ghost.

After thirty years, my mother had returned to Bridge Island.

# CHAPTER 8

"*H*ello." If the sight of her hadn't flooded me with memories of my childhood, the sound of her voice would have finished the job. It was the tone that got me. Like hearing an old song on the radio and being transported back to the memory of first hearing it. A love song that reminds you of your first kiss. A ballad that breaks your heart all over again.

The soft lullaby that lulled you to sleep in the middle of the night when a storm rattled the windows or cooed over your scraped knee.

"Hi, Marina, how are you?"

Her inquisitive eyes widened almost as much as her smile. She clapped her hands in a way I'd seen Aunt Ruth do when she was excited. So much more like a child than an adult.

"You know my name? That's so exciting!" She flipped in the water with a grace I envied, twisting as her body left the surface and returning on a swan dive. The mother I remembered had always moved like she was in water, while I clomped around and took corners too sharp. I'd been a mess of unexplained bruises from bumping into doorways or tripping over rugs.

The gawkiness of my preteen years never fully faded. Even as I watched her cut through the water with nary a splash, I rubbed at the dark spot forming above my elbow, tender though I had no memory of it happening.

"I know your name," I told her as she neared. "You used to live here." I pointed toward Bridge House, somewhat gratified to see that the lights dimmed a touch. I sensed the house's anticipation, a trepidation that mirrored my own. My stomach flipped and tumbled with an unpleasant mixture of adrenaline and acidity.

She reached a finger toward my tail, as if to run her hand along it, and I shifted. Rather than pull back, like an adult would if reacting to social cues, she let out a young giggle and moved closer.

"It's not polite to touch someone without asking permission." I used my Charley tone, the one that got my daughter's attention when she was a girl. Marina snatched her hand away and turned her face to mine.

"I'm sorry, I didn't mean to be rude. It's so rare I see others of my kind this close to the surface." That piqued my curiosity. Did that mean there were larger numbers far below? I hadn't yet swum deep enough to find the communities I'd heard existed at the bottom of the sea. Maybe I didn't want to. But there wasn't time to consider that, as Marina's fingers stroked the edge of my fins.

"It's so pretty. So different from mine." She flipped her tail toward me. "I thought perhaps it was what drew me here."

"What do you mean, it drew you here?" A strange wake of chills crossed my arms. Could the house call my mother all this time? Or was the lure of North Bridge what had brought her here?

"Oh, I was swimming ..." Her voice trailed, and her eyes followed the bend of the bay. "I don't know where I was. Out there. Really far. And I bumped into an old friend." She dropped her voice as if about to share a secret and lifted her lips into a mischievous grin. "He's a pirate, you know."

"I've met him." That sour sensation in my stomach tilted again. I knew what had brought her, even without her saying his name. Jean Lafitte causing trouble. Damn pirate.

"He's so charming." She batted her eyes like a cartoon princess. "He told me about this lovely area that I might enjoy. He said it was all lit up for the holidays. And those lights sure are pretty!" For a moment, her face dimmed. "But something shinier than the lights called me. I've been swimming and swimming, and I can't quite find it." She reached for my tail again. I circled her to keep her hand at bay. "I thought perhaps it was your tail. It's not though. But it does remind me of something."

My heart pounded in my chest. It seemed clear she didn't know who I was, and though that should have hurt, I was surprised to find myself relieved. Maybe six months ago, that would have caused an ache so deep I couldn't function. I would have questioned what it was about me that was so forgettable that my own mother didn't recognize my face.

But I'd changed. Transformed in so many ways that the old me couldn't conjure the same pain. And the mermaid in front of me was no more the mother who'd abandoned me than I was the woman whose husband had cheated on her. They were both in the past.

Misty, the caretaker of Bridge House and a damn good human, had an instinct for the lost and confused supernatural who came to the waystation. If she was looking for something, it was my legacy to help her find it. Then let her move on.

"Marina, I'd be happy to swim around the island and help you find what you're looking for."

A shimmer of tears filled her eyes, and before I could dodge it, my mother wrapped her wispy arms around me and pulled me into a surprisingly strong hug. Man, she had boundary issues.

She released me with the same force she'd brought me forward and took off toward Norbert's favorite sunning spot. I followed suit, trying to keep up with her. Even though I swam daily, she was far faster and much more agile. I didn't get to find out how

Norbert would react to my mother's return, as he wasn't at his spot.

He wasn't in any of the places I was used to seeing him, and for the next hour I alternated between flapping my fins to keep up with a sprinting Marina and guiding her toward the hidden nooks and crannies I'd found in my own wanderings. I wasn't sure what we were looking for, but then again neither was she.

It was near midnight when she finally paused, flipping onto the banks near Dimitri's cabin to bask under the moonlight. I was tempted to bring her to the cabin and suggest we rest, even though introducing Dimitri to my mother felt strange. I was out of breath, and my muscles were like lead. Even as I lifted my tail to heft it out of the water, it was more like hauling bricks than moving a part of my body.

"It's not here." Marina crossed her arms and pouted like a toddler. "That pirate is a liar."

"Lafitte is known for causing trouble, Marina." I chuckled beside her, patting her shoulder. "But from what I've seen, he rarely lies. He just … stretches the truth a little to get what he wants. What is it you're looking for? You know, aside from something shiny?"

"I'm not supposed to tell anyone." Marina ran her fingers through the sand, casting her eyes down. "He made me promise."

The chill returned to me, this time tickling its way up my spine as I realized why Lafitte had sent her to me, and what had drawn her here.

"Marina, are you looking for a gem?" Her hands stilled, only for a moment, but she didn't answer. I swallowed, trying to keep my tone neutral. "Perhaps a star?"

Her head snapped up, and her mouth formed an *o*. Then she bit her lip, shifting her eyes from side to side as if Lafitte might appear and catch her telling his secret. She nodded.

"Damn, I could have saved us a few hours." My heart dropped. "I've been looking for it, too, Marina. For a few months now."

"Oh." Marina's body slumped. "That's disappointing."

I sighed beside her, dipping my head back and propping myself on my forearms. On this side of the island, Bridge House wasn't able to block the stars. I gestured at the brilliance of the night sky. "At least we have these stars."

"You're very nice. You remind me of someone I knew once." She smiled, though it dipped a fraction, and in that moment my heart held still. Then she shook her head, as if shaking off a pesky fly. "You know what? I never asked your name!"

There was a sliver of disappointment. My mother had clearly either become really good at suppressing memories or didn't have the capacity for deep emotions. Either way, there was not going to be any sort of mother/daughter reunion tonight. She was here for the Star. Nothing else.

But why tonight? Why, when I was being visited by ghosts and supposed to learn some stupid lesson, had my mother appeared if not for us to reconcile the past? And yet, I still questioned my own acceptance of the situation. I had no desire to confront her, to spend the rest of the night going round and round over useless emotions. I didn't need to ask why she left. I already knew. And her behavior told me that in her time away, she'd embraced her mermaid fully. If there had ever been humanity in her, it was long gone.

She lifted her eyebrows, and I became aware that I was so lost in thought I'd never given her my name. Would it spark a memory? Would it matter at all? I extended my hand, the most human of gestures.

"Hi, Marina, I'm Misty. I grew up here, and I take care of Bridge Island, and all those who come to it."

A strange pressure filled the air, until I thought my ears would pop. My mother was so mermaid she had no idea what a handshake was, so she stared at my outstretched arm and waited for it to do something. She put her hands to her head, the only indication that she, too, felt the sudden swelling of the world around us.

"Misty." A single tear fell from her eye, shining under the

moon like a lone star. "There is one place we haven't looked. It's very secret. Can I show it to you?"

She leaped into the water and plunged straight down without waiting for my reply.

# CHAPTER 9

*T*he only time I'd gone this deep was the night Dimitri and Lucas fought over the bridge. Lucas had somehow commanded weird sea snakes to grab me and drag me down. I shuddered now at the memory, and the tang of their blood as they'd been ripped apart filled my mouth all over again.

Marina took me down even further, following the crevices that made up the island like a jagged trail. We had swum for at least an hour before I realized where we were headed.

She was taking me underneath the island.

It was so much deeper than I'd imagined. Though the area surrounding the island was relatively shallow, the waters here were encased in darkness. After a moment, my mermaid eyes adjusted. Marina paused and looked up, extending her hands as if presenting the world to me. I angled my body to take it in.

If a tree had spread roots that connected to nothing, and flourished in the middle of the ocean, this is what it would look like. Black rocks weaved this way and that, forming a foundation of stone and earth that seemingly grew from nothing. Along the base was a shimmering thin layer of a material I didn't recognize. I swam closer, running my finger along its smooth edges. It was like sand mixed with gold specks then packed close.

It rippled as if alive, filling me with the most glorious sensation, like the whole of creation was in front of me.

My little island floated on pure magic.

I wept at its beauty and would have stayed there staring the rest of my life if not for Marina. She grabbed me and shook, pointing toward the center. As we swam closer, my eyes adjusted again to a growing light.

It was hard to assess the exact location, but it seemed to be just below where Bridge House was built. A hidden cove that glowed so bright darkness disappeared. Marina launched herself into the cove, and I followed. We landed on more of the sand that was packed along the bottom of the island. For a reason I didn't understand, perhaps as simple as gravity, there was no water.

It smelled of damp air and fresh moss, though nothing grew in the crevices. Just large enough to fit the two of us comfortably, and only if we bent our tails and curled them under. Marina sat up straight, but I had to dip my head to keep from bonking it on the rock above me.

"Misty!" Her voice echoed in the small space, and her ensuing laugh was loud enough to cover the soft lapping of water at our fins.

She held her arms out and lifted her head. She hadn't been repeating my name.

Tiny drops of water filled the air, forming a cool, damp cloud around us.

"Oh! It's ... misty here." I reached for the mist, as if I could touch it. It dodged my fingers but landed on my skin like a million tiny specks of light.

"I came here once before." Marina wiped a sudden stream of tears from her cheeks. "I can't remember why, but I know I was here, and I was happy." She looked around the cove, lost in her own fractured memories. "It was Christmas Eve. And there was pain. And fear. But joy. So much joy."

She propped herself on her elbows, much like I'd done on the shores earlier, and bent her knees. Her tail faded, and she planted her feet. The lump in my throat grew into a sob. My teeth chattered through the rush of emotions overwhelming me.

"I found something precious here. Something so amazing and magical I knew it had the power to change my life." She sat upright with a sudden force and cradled her arms, looking down at them as if a baby might appear.

"It was mine and beautiful, but deep down I knew I couldn't keep it." Fresh tears flowed. Marina caught my face in her hands. "It belonged to the island, you see? It was meant for the island." Her fingers trailed my cheeks. Her pupils dilated in and out, as if she were in two places at once, both light and dark.

"I wanted it. Her? I wanted ... her. So much."

My throat clogged, and my heart broke. "I believe you."

"I had something precious, too. Something I'd found up there." She jabbed a finger toward the house above us. "I thought maybe if I traded my precious thing for the island's precious thing, it would let me keep her." She looked around for a moment, and her gaze stopped in the far corner. "I buried it."

I followed her gaze to the small mound untouched by light. She reached over and dug into it, murmuring words to herself I couldn't understand. Then she let out a high-pitched *a-ha* and held it up for me to see.

The gem dangled from a gilded chain so bright I shielded my eyes to take it in. A dozen pearls surrounded it like a warm hug from the ocean. The jewel in the center was the clearest I'd ever seen, so crystalline I could make out the expression of awe on my mother's face, though she was on the other side. I'd never seen an azure so perfect. Never a cyan so pure.

"You found it, Marina." My breath caught. My body trembled. Marina held Talia's Star.

"It didn't work, did it?" Marina lowered the star to search my face. "I didn't get to keep the precious thing, did I?"

"No, Marina, you didn't." I closed my eyes for a moment, swallowing until my mouth was no longer dry, until I could find the right words, any words, to convey the impossible.

I recognized the mixture of pain and pride on her face, and the swelling of my heart. I'd felt it before. When I'd dropped my daughter at college. When she'd gotten her first job in the art world. When she'd experienced her first heartbreak.

Marina did not remember that she was a mother, but she carried the scars of motherhood all the same.

"You know what, Marina? I'm not sure we're meant to keep the most precious things to ourselves. I think they are supposed to find themselves. And, if we're lucky, we get to see that discovery." I closed her hands over Talia's Star, bringing her knuckles to my lips. "But you can have this."

Maybe the light around us dimmed, or maybe I couldn't see clearly. It was hard to tell. Marina cupped the gem at her heart, cradling it. Her eyes were clear and bright. Her smile was full and untethered.

She mimicked my gesture, placing Talia's Star in my hands and kissing my fingertips.

"That's okay, Misty. I think this shining gem is right where it belongs." She squeezed my hands before releasing them and slid into the water. "Thank you so much for this adventure."

The glistening pink of the tips of her tail were the last I saw of my mother before she left the cove and swam away.

# CHAPTER 10

$\mathcal{B}$y the time I reached the shore, night was fading. A hazy pre-dawn cloud hovered over the rocks of Norbert's favorite sunning spot when I arrived. He still wore the cap, but it wasn't as ridiculous as I thought.

I dangled Talia's Star for him to see, enjoying his alligator grin. He nodded toward the levee that led up to Bridge House.

Walter stood with his back to the water, hat askew and eyes lifted. I wasn't sure how much longer I had with him, so I held onto my story to tell Norbert later and rushed to join him.

"The sun will rise soon." His voice was back on an even cadence, with a hint of the Kentucky accent he used to impersonate Lincoln.

"It always does," I told him. "Where did you disappear to?"

"Nowhere. Everywhere. I can't be sure." He jerked his head back toward the shore. "Your alligator friend found me. Did you know he can talk?"

"Sometimes he talks too much." I mock-glared down the sand at Norbert, whose eyes were entirely too innocent. It wouldn't surprise me if he'd known how to reach Walter the entire evening. "Walter, I'm so sorry that I blurted out your ... ghostliness ... the way I did. That was inconsiderate. Apparently, I was going through something of my own."

"I've had some time to digest it." Walter steepled his fingers with a deep nod. "I have found that it is not entirely safe, when one is misrepresented under his very nose, to allow this misrepresentation to go uncontradicted."

"That's very profound."

"Lincoln said that." Walter chuckled, and I joined him. "But I quite like the sentiment, don't you? Looking back, it was obvious the entire time. You only blurted, in your words, what deep down I'd known all along. In fact, I should thank you for pulling me from the oblivion of denial."

"Don't mention it." I shrugged my shoulders, clutching Talia's Star against my side. "What do you do now?"

"That is the question, isn't it?" Walter stroked his beard. "Have you gone through your thing?"

"I'm not sure," I finally answered. "I think I can at least see my thing more clearly. And I understand it better. Maybe there are things we never get over or move on from." I let out a sigh, releasing something like thirty years of emotional baggage in one big breath. "Maybe some things never get closure."

"Let it never be said that I lived for the future. Though my eyes could see forward, the past taught me to keep my heart rooted in the present."

"Another Lincolnism?"

"No." Walter removed his stovepipe hat, pressing it into his fingers. "That one was me."

He placed the hat back on his head and fiddled with his collar until his bowtie was straight. Then, he extended his hand to me, the most human of gestures. I shook it.

"I do hope I get to meet him, wherever I go. I have many questions about the real Mary Todd."

"I hope you do too, Walter." I brushed a speck of sand from his lapel.

Walter bowed, pressing his hand to his waist. I waved good-bye, watching as the sun rose, illuminating him until he disappeared on the path to North Bridge, like specks of light, a trick of the eye that was never really there.

# CHAPTER 11

*B*y the time I reached Bridge House, I didn't seem to mind that there were three times as many holiday lights as the night before. Nor did I mind the lovely shades of rose adorning the roof, and how they transitioned to ruby as they neared the porch, like an ombré of the past, present, and future. The steps hummed under my feet when I climbed them. I stopped for a moment to pat the banister.

"I bet it was nice for you to see her, too. Even if she was never really yours."

"To see who?" Dimitri sat on the swing, one foot crossed on the opposite knee. He wore a t-shirt of deep red over his least faded jeans, which I guess was his attempt at holiday attire. I was still damp from my swim, but he folded me into his arms and drew me in for a kiss.

"The ghost of Christmas past. And present. And the future, now that I think about it. She was all three. Kind of." He furrowed his brow like that didn't make sense, which I suppose was fair. "I'll tell you all about it after I change."

"Go fast. Everyone's waiting in the cafe."

"In the cafe?" I craned my neck toward the extended patio, but he blocked my view. "What's going on?"

43

"They won't tell me," he grumbled. "Once we saw Walter on the shore with Norbert, we called off the search. Iris instructed me to wait here until you came back and bring you to them."

His voice was gruff with an annoyance that amused me. When we'd first met, I thought he was grumpy because of Lucas. Then I thought he was grumpy because of me. Now that I knew he was grumpy because he was a troll, it no longer set me on edge. He was just being himself.

"I'll be fast." I kissed him again then ran up the stairs. When I reached my bedroom, I tucked Talia's Star under my mattress. "I trust you to tell me where we can keep it safe." The House didn't answer, but my balcony doors swung open. I laughed. "I'm not peeking."

I took a quick shower, and though it felt a bit trite, let myself assess my looks in the mirror. I didn't hate the me that stared back. In fact, I almost liked it. Sure, a bit of Botox and a new moisturizer would take a few years off, but what was the fun in fighting the inevitable?

Still, I made a note to ask about my skincare routine the next time I went to Illusion Square. After all, part of being human was taking care of yourself, and even mermaids got dry skin.

Dimitri was at the bottom of the stairs when I returned. He smiled at me and ran his fingers through his hair.

"You look really pretty."

A thousand qualifiers popped up in my head, and part of me wondered if that would ever stop. It seemed like I'd grown a lot, but my default thoughts were still to brush away compliments. Oh well. I could deal with that tomorrow.

"Thanks. Let's see what shenanigans our krewe is up to." I twined my fingers through his and let him lead me back outside.

When we rounded the corner, my heart swelled three sizes. All the cafe tables had been pulled together, and a festive red tablecloth was draped over them. A birthday banner took up the whole of one side, and red and silver balloons adorned the rest of the banisters.

The centerpiece was a beautiful mesh of flowers and some greenery I would never recognize, no doubt put together by Marilena in Illusion Square. But it spoke to me. The flowers weren't too frilly, with lovely pops of purple and yellow, and the deep green of the leaves served as an earthy contrast to their softness. In the middle was a cluster of lotus flowers as beautiful as my tail.

I touched it with tears in my eyes. Even if I watered it every day and put it in the perfect spot of sunlight, I was going to kill this work of art. It was inevitable.

The tears streamed harder when Sam stepped out of the kitchen, balancing the biggest cake I'd ever seen on a tray. His proud smile lit me up inside. Behind him were my people, each of them with plates of breakfast foods.

They brought them to the tables and set them down, singing as they went. Iris's lovely falsetto and Ruth's shrill timbre. Sam's hearty belt and Max's shockingly dulcet harmony. It was the most perfect chorus I'd ever heard.

Dimitri's hand tightened in mine. "It's your birthday?"

"Uhm ... yeah."

I avoided his gaze, moving forward to hug each and every one of my friends and family. Kitty poured mimosas and handed me a large mug of coffee. I heaped food on my plate, starving and wired from a night of swimming and emotion, but happy in a place down in my core.

For a moment, all the tiny voices that whisper about what might go wrong were quiet. And that peace was a happy sliver of bliss, even if it was temporary.

"I should have known you would remember." Ruth leaned over to rest her head on my shoulder.

"Well, if you'd asked, we could have told you sooner." Iris dipped her champagne glass in my direction. "Though I understand not wanting to age."

"I owe everyone at this table an apology. I've been such a grump. I never liked my birthday. Once I left the island, it got glossed over by Christmas, and I let it. Figured that was easier than thinking about how another year had passed without any word from my mom."

Forks were set down on plates and glasses placed on tables. I had the full attention of my chosen family.

"She visited the island last night. She ... didn't remember me." I turned to meet Aunt Ruth's eyes. "But she remembered enough to show me where I was born. A cove at the bottom of the island. Did you know about it?"

In her very Ruth way, her childlike demeanor faded just enough to remind me that a wise and wonderful woman lived underneath. Ruth, who'd brought me back here when I needed it, and who'd sacrificed so much for so many. Ruth, who'd always chosen joy and magic, even when pain lurked beneath the surface.

"The night you were born, Marina disappeared into the water and came back with you. It doesn't surprise me that's where she went to give birth. The most magical spot on the island was also her favorite. You could have drowned." Ruth drank from her mimosa as if she'd never had one before, making a sound of delight between each sip. "Say what you will about your mother, and there's a lot to be said, she knew how to live in the moment without worrying about the future."

"Not me." I grabbed the breakfast burrito on my plate with both hands. "I'm always thinking about tomorrow."

"They both matter." Iris reached across the table to take my hand, and I reluctantly dropped the burrito to squeeze hers. "The bits of the past that form us. The moments in the present that sustain us. The parts of the future that'll no doubt change us. It's okay to think about them all. How far you've come, where you are, and what you'll do next. You wouldn't be you if you didn't."

"That's true." I lifted the burrito and tore off a huge chunk, swallowing it down with a hearty sip of champagne. "I gotta be me."

# CHAPTER 12

*D*imitri was quiet throughout our breakfast feast, and disappeared while I was helping with the dishes. Since we'd never talked about spending Christmas together, I stayed at Bridge House with Ruth and Iris, opening presents and laughing into the afternoon.

Even Sam escaped from the kitchen to hang with us, unabashedly crying at the new apron I had had made for his large frame. And when I unwrapped my gift from Ruth, a shiny new tablet with our booking app installed and running, I sobbed right along with him.

Before dinner, I slipped out of the house and made my way to Dimitri's cabin under the bridge. He opened the door before I knocked, stopping in his tracks with a small box in-hand.

"I was on my way to see you."

"Beat ya to it." I shuffled my feet.

We stood there awkwardly, waiting for the other to speak. Then, of course, we both spoke at once.

"You could have told me—" He began.

"I wanted to explain—" I said.

With a chuckle and a dip of his head, I took his hand, and we strolled to the bench that overlooked the water. One of our favorite spots on the island. Though it kept our backs to the bridge and the house, I liked the idea that it offered a view of what might be headed toward us. Even if I couldn't see the future, at least it wouldn't sneak up on me.

Then again, maybe a few surprises weren't so bad.

"I'm sorry I didn't tell you it was my birthday." I nestled into his arm and threaded our fingers together. "I'm still not sure where we are in this relationship. And I it's been a long time since I was in one." I laughed and sat up, rotating to face him. "I have to re-learn how to romance."

Dimitri trailed his hand along my cheek, tucking a strand of hair behind my ear. He kissed my lips, whisper soft. "This relationship won't be like your last one, Misty."

His golden eyes blazed with a molten lava that swirled around inside me. Emotions, unidentified and terrifying, bolted into me.

"I brought you something." I tore myself away from his gaze to pull the bag from my pocket. "It's not your Christmas present. That's back at the house. I got you something, but then I didn't know if you got me anything, and then I overthought it and, well, now it's sitting in my bedroom."

"I get it." He broke through my rambling with a sharp kiss, then opened the bag, holding up the contents as if I didn't know what it was. "It's Talia's Star."

"It's a story I can't tell you tonight. Not because I don't want to but because I can't go through it all again. But I promise I will." I leaned into him, toying with the chain of the necklace. "I want you to hold onto it here."

He was quiet for a moment. When he spoke, the word broke. "Why?"

"Because you're safe." I pulled myself closer to him. "Lafitte will return for it. Hell, Lucas will probably come back, too. Who knows what else is waiting out there now that the bridge is restored, and we are back to full power. A thousand scenarios can happen on this wacky island we call home. And I'm not prepared for any of it, no matter how much I like to worry about it.

"But I know one thing with absolute assurance. You're on my side. Misty the Mermaid Caretaker of Bridge House and Dimitri the Golden Guardian of North Bridge." I looped my arms around Dimitri's neck and held tight. "We're a dynamic duo, who both happen to be pretty badass on our own."

His arms threaded around me, and we relaxed into each other. He separated and held a box up to me.

"I got you something, too. Not a Christmas present, though there's one of those for you at the cabin." He paused to smile. "This is your birthday gift."

I furrowed my brow. "Did you know, too?"

"No." He planted his hand on the back of his neck, casting his eyes away. "I made it this afternoon."

With trembling fingers, I lifted the lid of the box. Turquoise stones wrapped toward a bronze circle. Embedded in the circle was a compass. With a squeal of delight, I fastened it to my arm, turning round and round to watch the compass needle move.

"It won't move, not when you're on the island." Dimitri stood with me, turning me in a slow circle like a dance. "The whole thing is waterproof. You know, so you can swim with it on. But the compass is special."

I stared at the compass, then back at Dimitri. Only then did I notice that the pattern on the compass matched his eyes. He took my hand and held the bracelet up beside his face.

"It will always point to the island. Specifically, to the Bridge that will bring you back home."

"So, you *did* get some power when you took command." I grinned and held my arm close to my heart.

He put his fingers to his lips with a wink that made me laugh. I leaned into him.

"I hoped it might help you worry less about tomorrow. No matter what happens, Misty, you'll be able to find your way back." He wrapped himself around me. "Happy birthday, Misty."

"Merry Christmas, Dimitri."

I kept it to myself, even though I knew he'd understand, but I hoped it would never be more than a gorgeous bracelet. A talisman that reminded me that my compass wouldn't move. Because, at the end of the day, it pointed to me. To the place where I belonged. To the home that I'd created.

But if that changed, well ...

I knew I could cross that bridge when I got there.

THANK you for reading *Murky Midlife Waters*! I'm saying goodbye to Bridge Island, for now. But the town of Treater's Way is about to get a new resident, and she's got a lot to learn.

**It's never too late to find your voice. Especially when magic gets involved.**

48-year-old Simone Bardot's life is a junk drawer of a mess. Her husband is having an affair. Her son barely talks to her. And her therapy practice is failing.

But a mysterious inheritance is about to change everything. As long as she's willing to return to the hometown she avoided for thirty years to claim it.

**Read Now**

^^^ Scan the code above or click here to read Witchful Shrinking, the full-length first book in the engaging new paranormal women's fiction series *Midlife at the Magnolia.*

WHEN A CLUMSY DRAGON turns out to be her scorching hot ex, will an independent therapist reignite an old spark or let it smother?

^^^ To find out more, scan the code above or click here to claim your copy of *Not Yet Old Flames,* a Paranormal Women's Fiction romantic short, when you join my newsletter.

# ACKNOWLEDGMENTS

To being a cynic, but occasionally letting yourself be sappy. To the folks who live in the future, those who live in the past, and those who live in the moment. There's a place for you on Bridge Island.

# ABOUT JB LASSALLE

JB (Jen) Lassalle is a writer of later-in-life fantasy and low-steam romantic fantasy. She likes strong females, dimensional males, and found family friendships that triumph over nuanced bad guys you love to hate.

Jen is a New Orleans resident. The city, and the surrounding areas, serve as a rich backdrop for a world where magic exists and mystical creatures are not only real, but live among us.

When Jen isn't writing, she's hanging at a local park or coffee shop. She likes working out, which is kind of weird, loves yoga, and plays video games. Of course, she reads.

Jen and her husband have two kids. One is an avid competitive swimmer (which sucks up all their weekend time). The other is a daydreamer like Jen who plays the Mega Man theme on his guitar like a boss.

Jen isn't great with social media, but you can connect with her below. Or, join her newsletter when you claim your copy of *Not Yet Old Flames*, a second-chance Paranormal Women's Fiction romantic novella.

facebook.com/jblassalle

instagram.com/jblassalle

Made in the USA
Las Vegas, NV
16 November 2024

11950653R00038